Watch out for the shark!

Ariel brings Flounder to her secret grotto.

Ariel shows her treasures to Scuttle the seagull.

Scuttle tells funny stories.

Sebastian the crab leads King Triton's underwater orchestra.

Help Ariel and Flounder follow the musical notes to reach Sebastian.

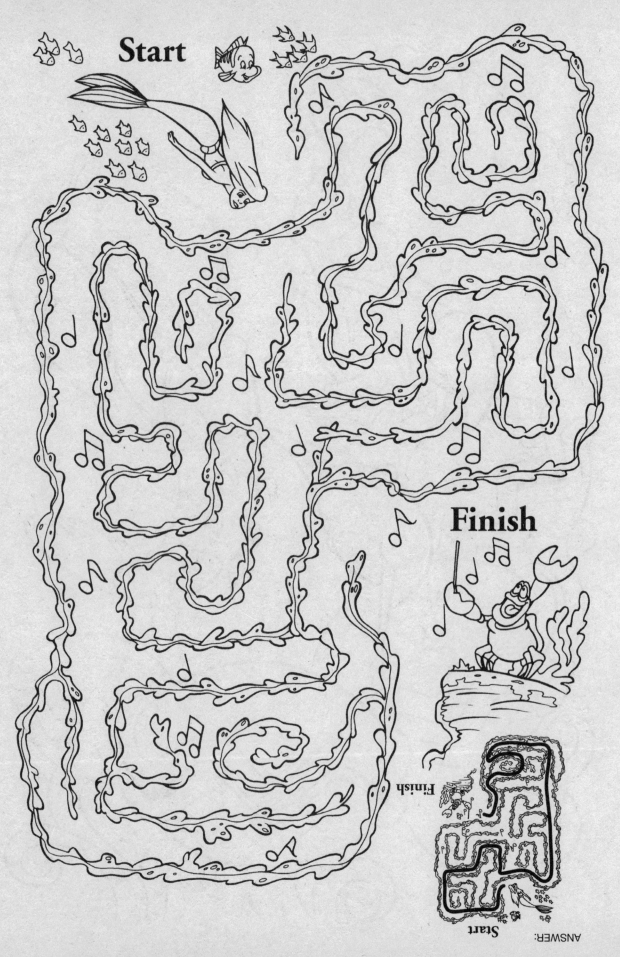

Start

Finish

Ariel's sisters are singing for their father.

The star of the show is missing!

Ariel follows a ship.

Ariel loves watching Prince Eric.

Prince Eric has fun aboard his ship.

The statue looks just like Prince Eric.

Ariel wishes on a star.

When Prince Eric's ship sinks, the little mermaid rescues him.

Ariel brings the statue of Eric to her secret grotto.

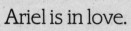

Ariel is in love.

King Triton tells Ariel to stay away from humans.

Ariel's father destroys her statue.

Look at this picture for one minute.
Then turn the page to see if you can spot eight differences.

© Disney

Ariel wants to look her best when she sees Prince Eric again.

Ursula is a sea witch.

Ursula watches Ariel and Flounder in her magic bubble.

Ariel wants to be human.

Ariel makes a deal with the sea witch.

Flounder and Sebastian watch as Ariel's tail
magically transforms into legs.

Ariel is excited to try out her new legs on land.

Prince Eric's dog, Max, finds Ariel on the beach.

How many 3-letter words can you make from the letters in
THE LITTLE MERMAID?

Ariel dances with Prince Eric.

Ariel takes Prince Eric for a wild ride.

Prince Eric thinks it's charming when Ariel combs her hair with a fork.

Max spots Sebastian on the dinner table.

Prince Eric and Ariel enjoy a lovely evening.

Oh, no! Vanessa tricks Eric into thinking he is in love with her.

Scuttle discovers that Vanessa is really Ursula!

Help Ariel find her way to Eric.

Finish

Start

ANSWER:

Flounder helps Ariel get to the ship.

Ariel's friends help Prince Eric.

King Triton rescues Ariel from the sea witch.

Prince Eric wants to marry Ariel.

What a beautiful bride!

Ariel and Eric say "I do!"

King Triton gives the bride a hug.

Ariel tosses her bouquet.

Sebastian and Flounder congratulate the happy couple.

Eric and Ariel dance for the first time as husband and wife.

Time to cut the cake!

King Triton is happy his daughter has found true love.

What a special day!

Prince Eric kisses his bride.

Ariel loves being a princess.

Prince Eric gives Ariel a special gift.

Look closely at the picture on the previous page.
Can you spot five things that are different on this page?

Sebastian and Ariel are ready for some fun.

Ariel goes for an exciting ride with her sister.

Flounder does a trick.

Ariel has something special to show Flounder.

Connect the dots to see what Ariel and Flounder have found.

Look at all the treasure!

Ariel gives Scuttle a pretty pearl.

Ariel loves her dinglehopper.

Ariel spends time with her underwater friends.

Ariel daydreams about Prince Eric.

"He loves me. He loves me not."

Ariel hugs Flounder.

Sebastian gets a kiss.

Circle the picture of Flounder that is different.

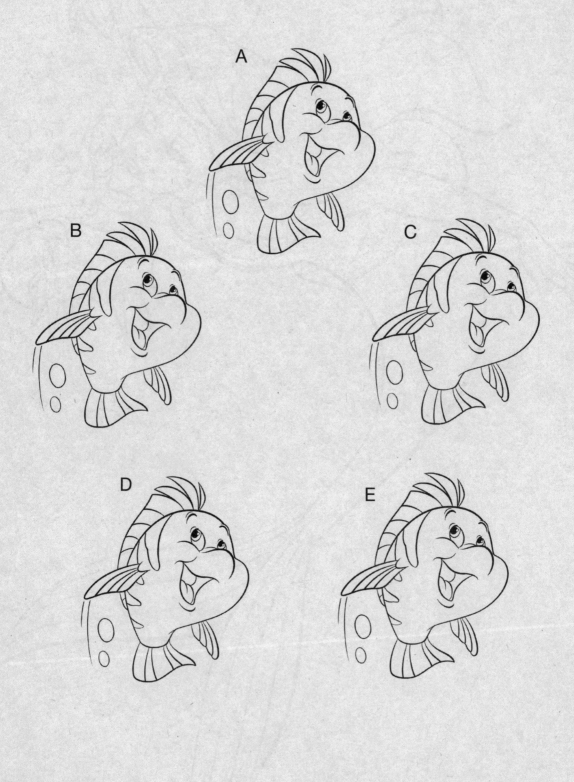

A

B

C

D

E

How many fish can you find?

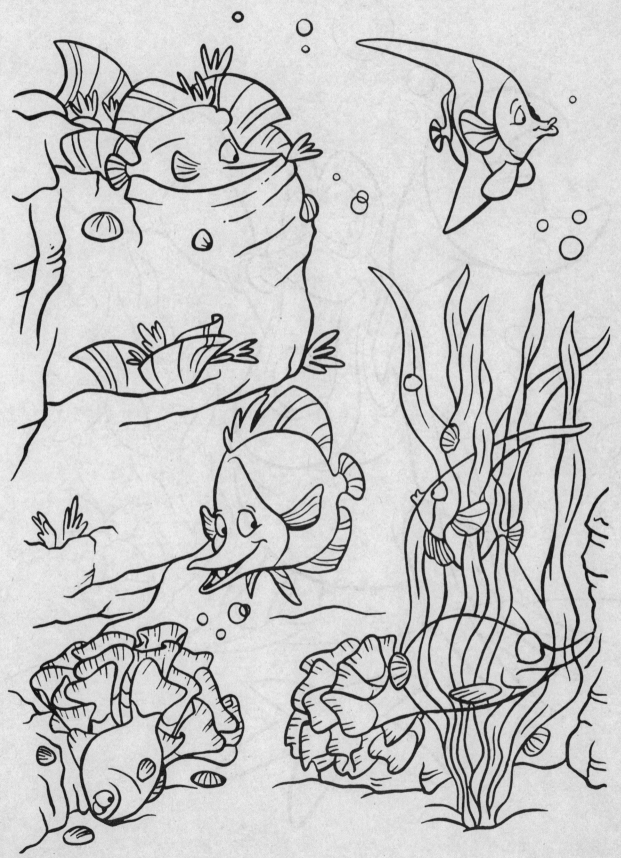

Hello, Sebastian!

Sebastian leads the way.

Ariel loves making music with her friends.

Time to rest.

Which line will lead Ariel to Flounder?

It's fun being a mermaid!

Flounder and Sebastian come up with an idea.

Underwater flowers make a nice surprise.

Ariel dreams about Eric.

Prince Eric surprises Ariel with a pet horse.

Ariel names her horse Beau.

Beau gets a yummy treat.

Scuttle flies over to meet Beau.

Ariel has a gift for Scuttle.

What did Ariel give Scuttle?
To find out, follow the lines and write each letter in the correct box.

WBEOGNOLSA

Ariel meets some cuddly friends.

What a snuggly bunny!

Can you lead the bunny to Ariel?

START

FINISH

ANSWER:

Ariel and Max go to the water's edge to visit with Flounder.

Ariel chats with a dolphin.

Sebastian and Ariel make a sand castle together.

Rowing is hard work for a little crab!

"My love for you is as big as the ocean!"